MR PERCY'S MAGIC GREENHOUSE

STORY BY ANTHEA KEMP

ILLUSTRATED BY PENNY METCALFE

LYNX
LONDON
1988

Mr Percy and Pumpkin
had a secret
at the bottom of their garden.

Down the garden path they went.
"Chilly this morning," said Mrs Maggs,
who was hanging out her washing.
"Nice and warm in your greenhouse, I expect."
Mr Percy just smiled and nodded.

From the outside
it looked just like any other greenhouse.

From the inside, too, it looked like
any other greenhouse – full of flowers:
pink ones that hung, blue ones that clung,
purple pom-poms in profusion,
and even a pomegranate in a big pot.
Mr Percy closed the door, winked at Pumpkin,
and said the magic words:
"MUNGO JUNGO, MANGO JANGO, JING JANG JONG."
Then everything began to change.

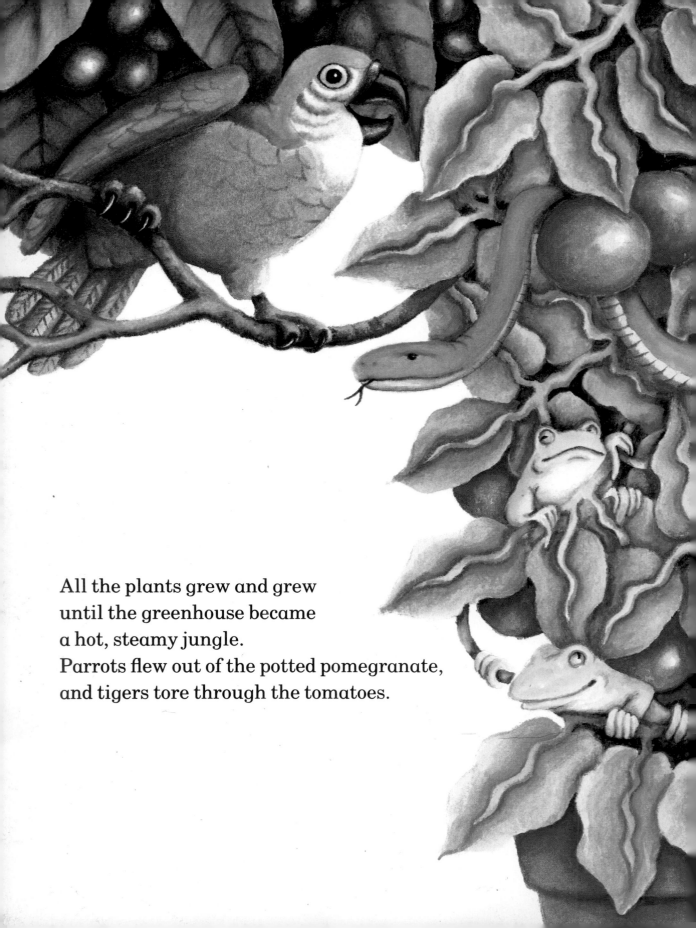

All the plants grew and grew
until the greenhouse became
a hot, steamy jungle.
Parrots flew out of the potted pomegranate,
and tigers tore through the tomatoes.

"Morning!" roared the tigers.
"Come for the boat again?"
"Yes," said Mr Percy,
"we're collecting mangoes for mango jam."
"Ah, mangoes," growled the tigers, licking their lips,
"they're mighty difficult to find."

They helped Mr Percy and Pumpkin into the boat,
which was tied to a banana tree
with terrible tiger knots.
Then Mr Percy and Pumpkin rowed off
down the jungly green river.

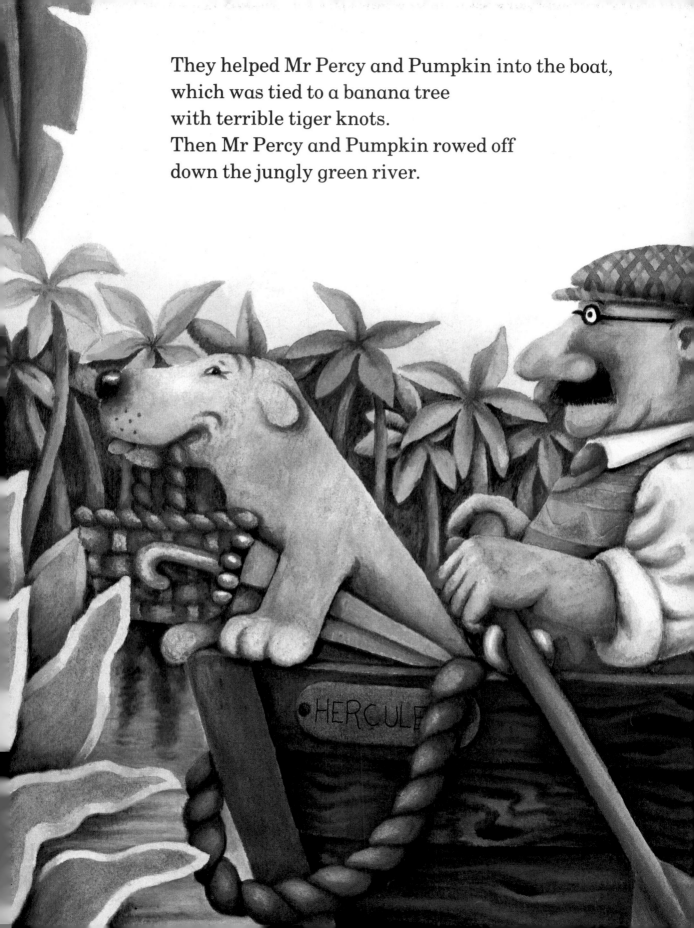

"Hello Pumpkin," trumpeted two elephants,
"come in and have a bath – you need one!"

"No fear!" barked Pumpkin,
who hated baths.

Around the next corner
some happy hippos were making a terrible din.
"Oh no," said Mr Percy,
"hippopotamuses never look where they're going
when they sing.
Hold tight, Pumpkin."

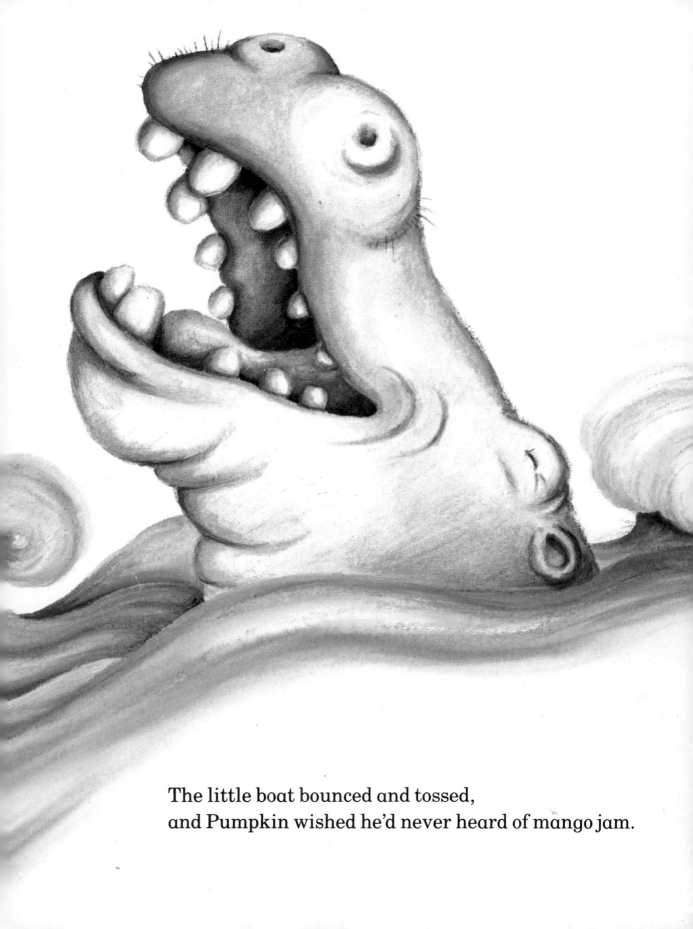

The little boat bounced and tossed,
and Pumpkin wished he'd never heard of mango jam.

Lounging on a branch was a languorous lion.
"Excuse me for disturbing you," said Mr Percy
politely, "which way are the mangoes?"
The lion looked down his nose at them,
and haughtily pointed one paw.
"Downriver," he yawned,
"if you're lucky."

On they rowed
until they met a bunch of dizzy fruit-bats,
hanging from the trees.
"Mangoes?" the fruit-bats chorused.
"Go this way – that way – over there!"
Mr Percy was so busy trying to decide which way to go
he didn't notice the boat drifting towards some logs.

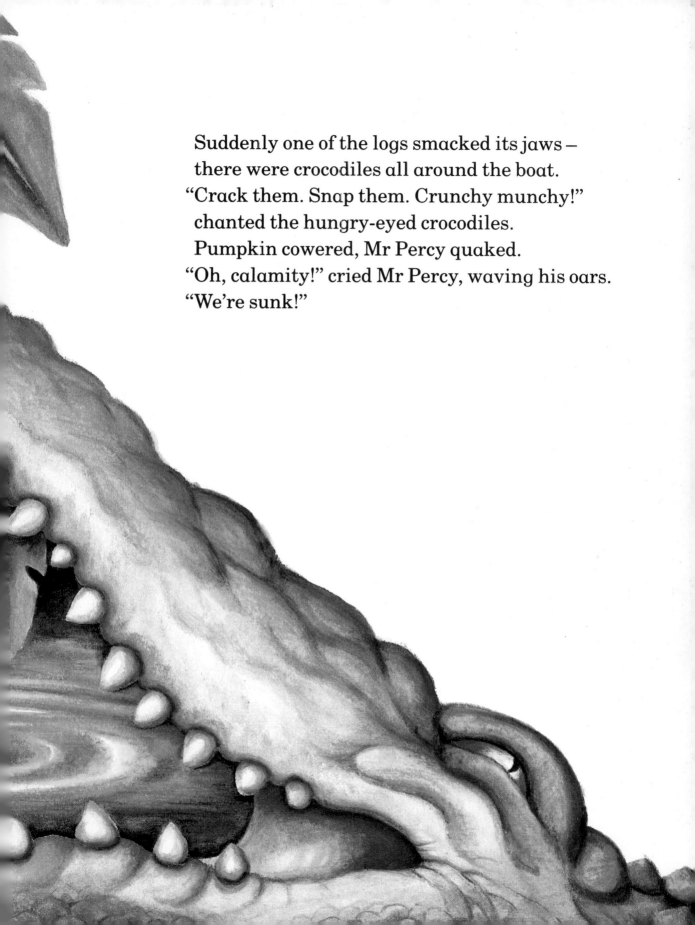

Suddenly one of the logs smacked its jaws —
there were crocodiles all around the boat.
"Crack them. Snap them. Crunchy munchy!"
chanted the hungry-eyed crocodiles.
Pumpkin cowered, Mr Percy quaked.
"Oh, calamity!" cried Mr Percy, waving his oars.
"We're sunk!"

But just then...
a troupe of mischievous monkeys
came swinging through the creepers,
hurling fruit and nuts in all directions.
Bruised and sticky,
the crocodiles slid sulkily away.
Mr Percy and Pumpkin were delighted –
not only were they saved,
but they had their mangoes, too.

Back at the banana tree,
the tigers were waiting to tie up the boat again
with terrible tiger knots.
"You found the mangoes!" they roared in surprise.
"No trouble at all," said Mr Percy.
"We'll bring you some jam next time. Goodbye."
"Goodbye," growled the tigers, waving their tails.

"JONG JANG JING, JANGO MANGO, JUNGO MUNGO."
Mr Percy said his magic words,
backwards of course,
and there they were back in their greenhouse.

It looked like any other greenhouse,
except for a big basket
overflowing with strange and luscious fruit.

"Evening, Mr Percy," called Mrs Maggs,
who was taking in her washing.
"You spend ever such a lot of time in your
greenhouse. What on earth do you find to do?"
Mr Percy just smiled a secretive smile.
"Have a mango," he said.

Text copyright © Anthea Kemp 1986
Illustrations copyright © Penny Metcalfe 1986

First published in Great Britain in 1986
by Victor Gollancz Ltd
This Lynx edition published in 1988
by Victor Gollancz Ltd, 14 Henrietta Street, London WC2E 8QJ

British Library Cataloguing in Publication Data
Kemp, Anthea
Mr Percy's magic greenhouse.
I. Title   II. Metcalfe, Penny
823'.914 [J]

ISBN 0 575 04341 5

Printed and bound in Hong Kong by Imago Publishing Ltd